GLITTER
TATTOO STORIES

Glitter
Tattoo
Fun!

The Mermaids' Ball

By Bea Sloboder
Illustrated by Heidi Petach

With best fishes to Ronnie, Victoria, Yvette,
and the rest of the great group at Grosset!—H.P.

Grosset & Dunlap • New York

All the little mermaids stretch and yawn. It's time to swim out of their oyster beds. It's time to get ready for the Mermaids' Ball!

At breakfast they sip seaweed tea, while they make plans for a busy, busy day.

First they must go shopping for something special
to wear. Each mermaid wants to look her best for the ball.

At the Old Shipwreck Shop, they find a treasure chest.
It's filled to the brim with sparkling jewels—just the thing!

Now it's off to the coral reef. The mermaids pick out colorful coral to put in their hair. There's pretty seaweed, too, and shells of every shape and size!

After their shopping trip, the mermaids lounge in the lagoon, and take a relaxing bath in the warm water.

The waterfall is perfect for washing their long, long hair.
But they don't need to blow-dry it for an undersea ball!

Now the mermaids get dressed. They decorate themselves with all the wonderful things they have found.

How beautiful they are!

Off they go to the ball in a conch-shell coach, drawn by six elegant seahorses.

When they arrive at the castle, the mermaid queen comes out to greet them. "Come in, come in!" she says. "The Mermaids' Ball is ready to begin!"

The orchestra plays their favorite tunes. The mermaids wave their arms and swish their tails. They dance the night away!

Dancing makes them as hungry as can be—just in time for the royal feast!

The chef dishes out delicacies from the sea—*sand*wiches, *sponge* cake, and *water*melon!

The Mermaids' Ball is drawing to a close. But first—
a grand bubbleworks display!
The mermaids watch with delight as colorful bubbles
fill the ballroom and burst over their heads.

What fun the mermaids have had at the Mermaids' Ball!

The Flower Princesses

By Elizabeth Anders
Illustrated by Jerry Smath

To Emily and Maggie—J.S.

Grosset & Dunlap • New York

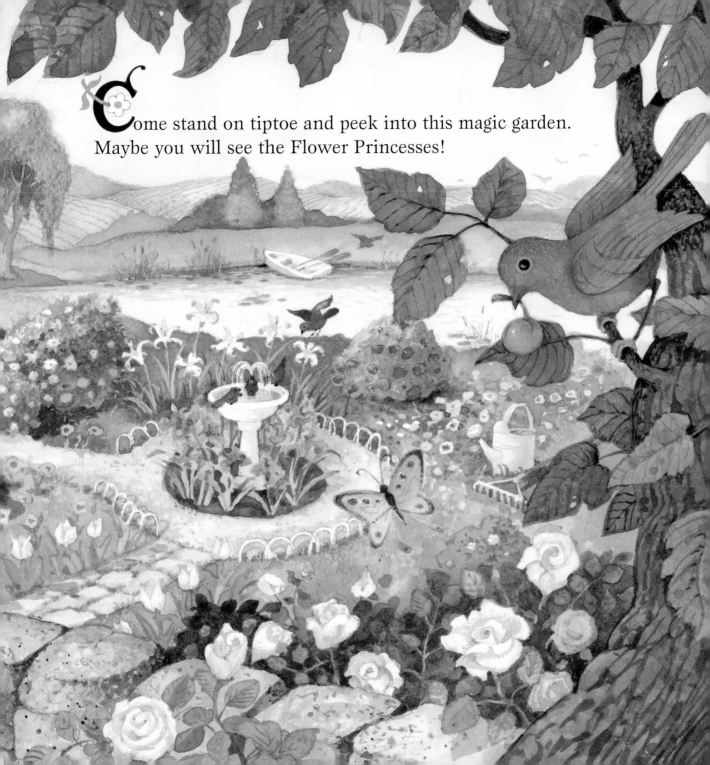

ome stand on tiptoe and peek into this magic garden.
Maybe you will see the Flower Princesses!

There they are—Princess Buttercup, Princess Hyacinth, Princess Iris, Princess Lily, Princess Tulip, and Princess Rose. Can you see them playing in the grass? They are as tiny as fairies!

The Flower Princesses love to laugh
and sing and play games together.

But each princess has something special she likes to do, all by herself.

Princess Buttercup, in her bright yellow dress, likes to skip to the meadow. There, she runs and plays with the butterflies, gathering buttercups until her basket is full.

Princess Hyacinth sits in a berry bush, drinking from dewdrops and listening to the bluebirds sing.

Princess Iris has a peapod canoe. She paddles around the fountain all day long, splashing as she goes.

Princess Lily likes to spend her days
at the pond. Watch her leap across the
lily pads, playing tag with the frogs!

Princess Tulip is a dancer. She whirls and twirls on her tiny feet, moving to the music of the wind.

Last is Princess Rose, riding a dragonfly
through the air. She swoops and glides over
the garden, waving to her sisters.

When the day is almost over, and the sun is starting to set, it is time for the Flower Princesses to have a tea party.

As the moon and stars come out, the Flower
Princesses go to sleep in their little flower beds.

Now, what do you think Flower Princesses
dream about?

Fluttery Butterflies

**By Tennant Redbank
Illustrated by Sonja Lamut**

Grosset & Dunlap • New York

Five shimmering butterflies
flutter across the sky.

Here is a blue butterfly...
a purple butterfly...
a red butterfly...
and a green butterfly.

Butterflies can be just one color
or lots of different colors.

A hungry bird flies over the meadow.
The butterflies hide.
Can you find six butterflies here?

Butterflies love to land on flowers.
They sip the nectar.
It's their breakfast!

Dark clouds roll in.
They cover the sky.

It starts to rain.
Where does a butterfly go in the rain?

Maybe under a leaf.

The rain stops.
There is one rainbow in the sky
and another rainbow
of colorful butterflies!

One butterfly lands
on the very tip
of a blade of grass.

Butterflies are so light,
the blade of grass
does not even bend!

Soon the day is over.
Where do butterflies go at night?

Some rest in the tall grass.

The next morning,
the butterflies come out.
They warm their wings in the sun.
Then they fly off, looking for flowers
to land on today.

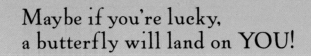

Maybe if you're lucky,
a butterfly will land on YOU!

Busy Ballet School

By Emily Sollinger
Illustrated by Stacey Lamb

For Mom and Dad—E.S.

GROSSET & DUNLAP • New York

Today is the first day of ballet school. I can hardly wait! I pack my ballet bag and get ready to go. In my bag, I put my ballet slippers, leg warmers, and a ribbon to tie my hair.

the nutcracker

When I get there, I am excited and a little nervous. I see a friend.
"Hi! I am so glad that you are starting ballet school, too," I tell her.
We walk together down the hall toward the studio. Our teacher is
standing in the doorway, ready to greet us.

First we learn the five positions.

First position.

Second position.

Third position.

Fourth position.

Fifth position.

After the five positions, it's time to move on to the barre.
We learn the tendue. This is really just a fancy word for pointing your toe on the floor.
We also learn how to hold and move our arms softly and gracefully.

We stop to take a break. It is very important
to drink lots of water during ballet class.

Now we learn different kinds of turns. First we put our hands on our shoulders. We learn how to spot ourselves in the mirror. When you spot, you keep your eyes on one thing—like the mirror, or a poster on the wall. That way you don't get dizzy.

Our teacher walks over to the corner of the room.
e asks everyone to come over. "This is the imagination trunk,"
e says. She opens up the top of a large trunk. Inside are all sorts
magical things. There are colored feathers, different kinds of
oth, wands, instruments, and costumes. It's amazing!

"Now I want each one of you to choose something from the trunk and use your imagination! You can be anything."
"I am a bird!" yells Megan as she flaps her arms and waves purple feathers.

"I am a fairy princess," I sing while
waving my magic wand.

"I am an elephant," roars Sam,
swinging his arms back and forth.

It's time to make a circle. We all hold hands and move in a circle. When the teacher changes the music, we switch directions and go the other way.

Next we practice leaping. We go across the floor—one by one. Run, run, run, run, and LEAP!

At the end of a class or a show, a ballerina always curtsies.
A curtsy is a special ballet bow. The boys do regular bows.

Class is over! We all clap for each other
and for our teacher. I love ballet school!